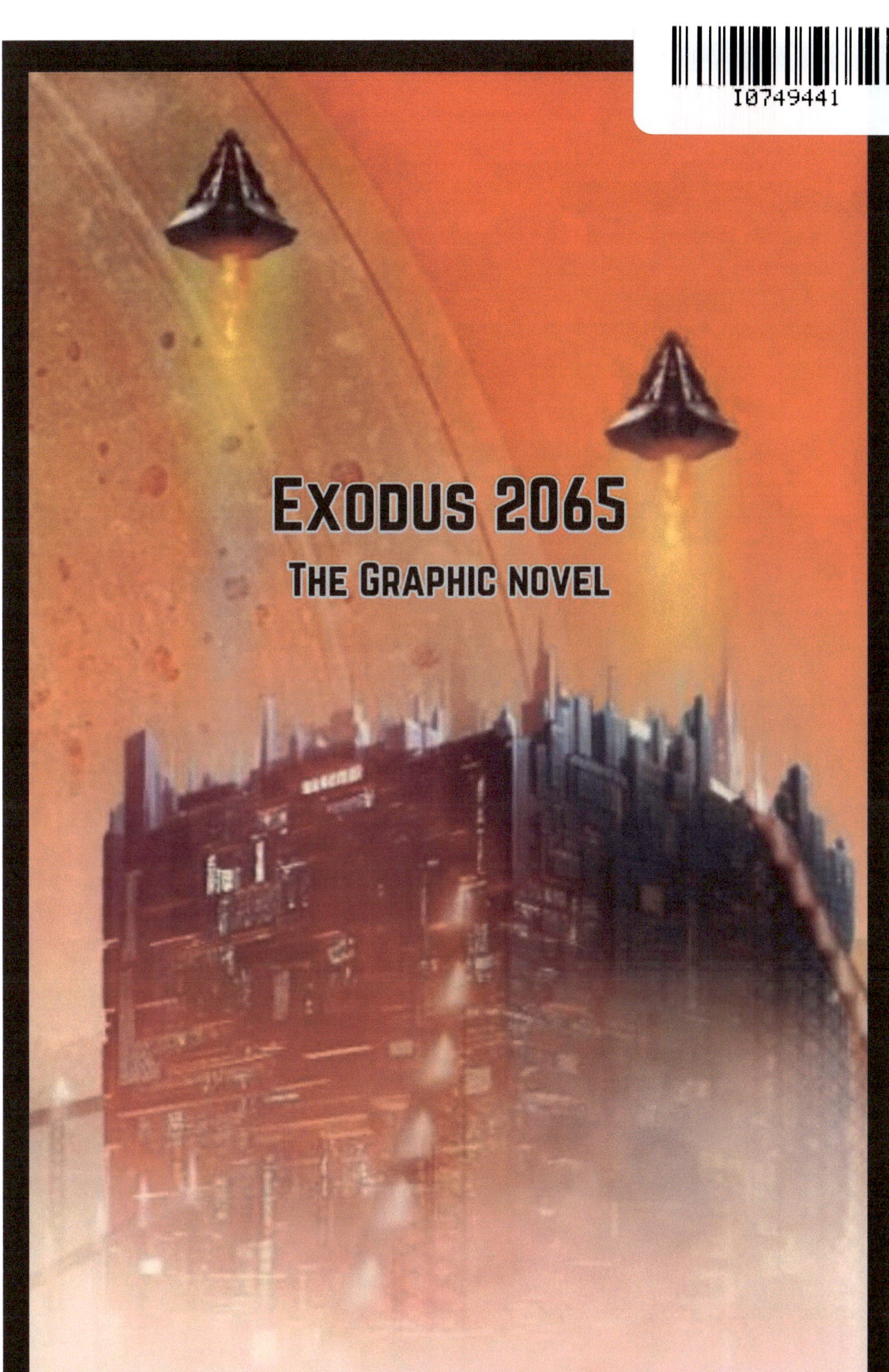
EXODUS 2065
THE GRAPHIC NOVEL

Exodust 2065

The Graphic novel

By Zack Samo

Zack Samo Books

Exodus 2065

Graphic Novel Adaptation of the Sci-Fi Novel Exodus 2065

Written and Created by Zack Samo

For permissions, inquiries, or other matters, please contact:
zacksamobooks@gmail.com

Published by Zack Samo Books

To my father,
who taught me the courage to face my demons,
both within and without.
I miss you every day,
but your strength and love remain my guiding light.

PROLOGUE

2045

THE GREAT QUAKE, THE STRONGEST EARTHQUAKE EVER RECORDED IN HUMAN HISTORY. THE QUAKE LASTED FOR AN HOUR, SHAKING THE CITY TO ITS FOUNDATIONS AND CAUSING A TSUNAMI THAT CLAIMED CLOSE TO TWO MILLION LIVES.

NEW LOS ANGELES, CALIFORNIA, A CITY ONCE CONSIDERED A MARVEL OF ENGINEERING AND A SYMBOL OF HUMANITY'S RESILIENCE. BUILT FROM THE ASHES OF THE FORMER CITY THAT WAS DESTROYED BY THE GREAT QUAKE OF 2045.

THE WORLD'S GREATEST MINDS AND ENGINEERS CAME TOGETHER TO REBUILD THIS CITY AS A UTOPIAN DREAM. IT TOOK OVER TWO DECADES AND COST FIFTY TRILLION DOLLARS, BUT THE RESULT WAS A GIANT CUBE CITY, ONE HUNDRED AND THIRTY STORIES HIGH AND COVERING 150 SQUARE MILES.

MAGWAYS BUSTLING WITH MILLIONS OF MAG MOBILES, FLYING VEHICLES THAT COULD REACH SPEEDS OF 150 MILES AN HOUR.

HOWEVER, NOW, NEW L.A. LOOKS LIKE A GHOST TOWN. NO ACTIVITY, NO FLYING VEHICLES, NO BUSTLING CITY LIFE. THE ONCE-GLORIOUS CITY HAS BECOME A HAUNTING REMINDER OF THE DEVASTATION BROUGHT BY THE A.D. EVENT.

ON FEBRUARY 25TH, ***ASTEROID DMN669*** HIT EARTH.

2065

PULVERIZED 150 MILLION PEOPLE AND WIPED INDONESIA OFF THE MAP, LEAVING BEHIND A 400-MILE WIDE IMPACT CRATER. THE ASH AND DEBRIS HUNG IN THE UPPER ATMOSPHERE, BLOCKING THE SUN FOR THREE MONTHS AND CAUSING DARKNESS FOR THE ENTIRE PLANET

650-FOOT HIGH WALL OF WATER SLAMMED AGAINST THE WORLD. NEW L.A. AND OTHER CITIES BUILT LIKE IT, WITH FLOOD DIVERTING SYSTEMS, SUFFERED LESS DAMAGE. CITIES BUILT THE OLDER WAY, WERE SUBMERGED UNDER OCEAN WATER

THE SHOCKWAVES FROM THE IMPACT SENT MILLIONS OF TONS OF ROCKS, DEBRIS, AND ASH HUNDREDS OF MILES INTO SPACE, CREATING A RING OF DEBRIS AROUND EARTH LIKE SATURN. THE IMPACT KNOCKED EARTH OUT OF ITS ORBIT, CLOSER TO THE SUN. MORE THAN A THIRD OF THE POPULATION DIED.
THE EARTH WAS NO LONGER THE SAME. THE ASTEROID IMPACT HAD SHIFTED IT CLOSER TO THE SUN AND CAUSED THE MAJOR FAULT LINES TO WIDEN AND EXTEND BY MILES
THE INTENSE HEAT HAD UNLEASHED CREATURES FROM THE DEPTHS OF THE EARTH, GARGOYLE-LIKE DEMONS WITH RAZOR-SHARP TEETH AND CLAWS THAT COULD RIP A MAN APART WITH ONE SWIPE.
...FEW MONTHS LATER...
HUMANITY HAD BEEN ON A MISSION TO ESCAPE THIS DYING PLANET FOR YEARS, BUT AS THE DEMONS STARTED TO OVERWHELM THE FIRST DEFENSIVE WALLS AROUND THE FAULT LINES, THE URGENCY TO LEAVE BECAME EVEN GREATER.

THEY QUICKLY REALIZED THAT ONE WALL WOULD NOT BE ENOUGH TO PROTECT AGAINST A MASSIVE DEMON ATTACK. SO, THEY CONSTRUCTED A SECOND WALL, HALF A MILE FROM THE FIRST. THIS WALL WAS A MASSIVE FEAT OF ENGINEERING, TOWERING 66 FEET HIGH AND 16 FEET WIDE, MADE FROM AN IMPENETRABLE BLEND OF CARBON STEEL AND TITANIUM ALLOYS.

HUMANITY HAD BEEN ON A MISSION TO ESCAPE THIS DYING PLANET FOR YEARS, WITH THE GOVERNMENTS OF THE WORLD BUILDING GIANT SPACESHIPS KNOWN AS **ARKS** TO EVACUATE AS MANY PEOPLE AS POSSIBLE.

IN THE CHAOS AND RUSH TO ESCAPE, LT. COLONEL **ADAMU** FOUND HIMSELF FACING A DILEMMA. HE WAS DETERMINED TO STAY BEHIND, BUT HE HAD A 21-YEAR-OLD DAUGHTER, **RAMIA**, TO CONSIDER.

SHE WAS THE ONLY FAMILY HE HAD LEFT AFTER THE PASSING OF HIS WIFE YEARS BEFORE. HE DIDN'T KNOW HOW HE WAS GOING TO TELL HER THAT HE WAS STAYING BEHIND TO FACE THE UNKNOWN DANGERS ON A DYING PLANET.

-CHAPTER 01-
OPERATION EXODUS 2065

SHE DOESN'T KNOW YET... SHE WOULDN'T UNDERSTAND WHY I HAVE TO STAY...
VROOMMM
VRRRRR
WELL, WELL, WELL... LOOKS LIKE WE'VE GOT OURSELVES A HERO...
YOU'RE ALL ALONE.. SILVER BOY. WHAT MAKES YOU THINK YOU CAN PROTECT THIS CITY BY YOURSELF?
VRRROOOSH
HARD TO KEEP UP WITH THE OLD MAN
STILL..

...I admit it. You still got it, dad.
Of course I do!
Don't get carried away in your old age, now.

Happy Birthday, Dad.
Thanks
66 now, right?
Not that old Ramia, not that old

How are you, Jake?
I'm good, Adamu You're looking good too, for 38
You're becoming more like Ramia
HAHAHA!!

Dad, Jake and I have been working on a gift for you for the past year. We wanted to give it to you under different circumstances, but knowing how much you dislike surprises, I hope you like it

Dorothy, open the garage door
What is it?

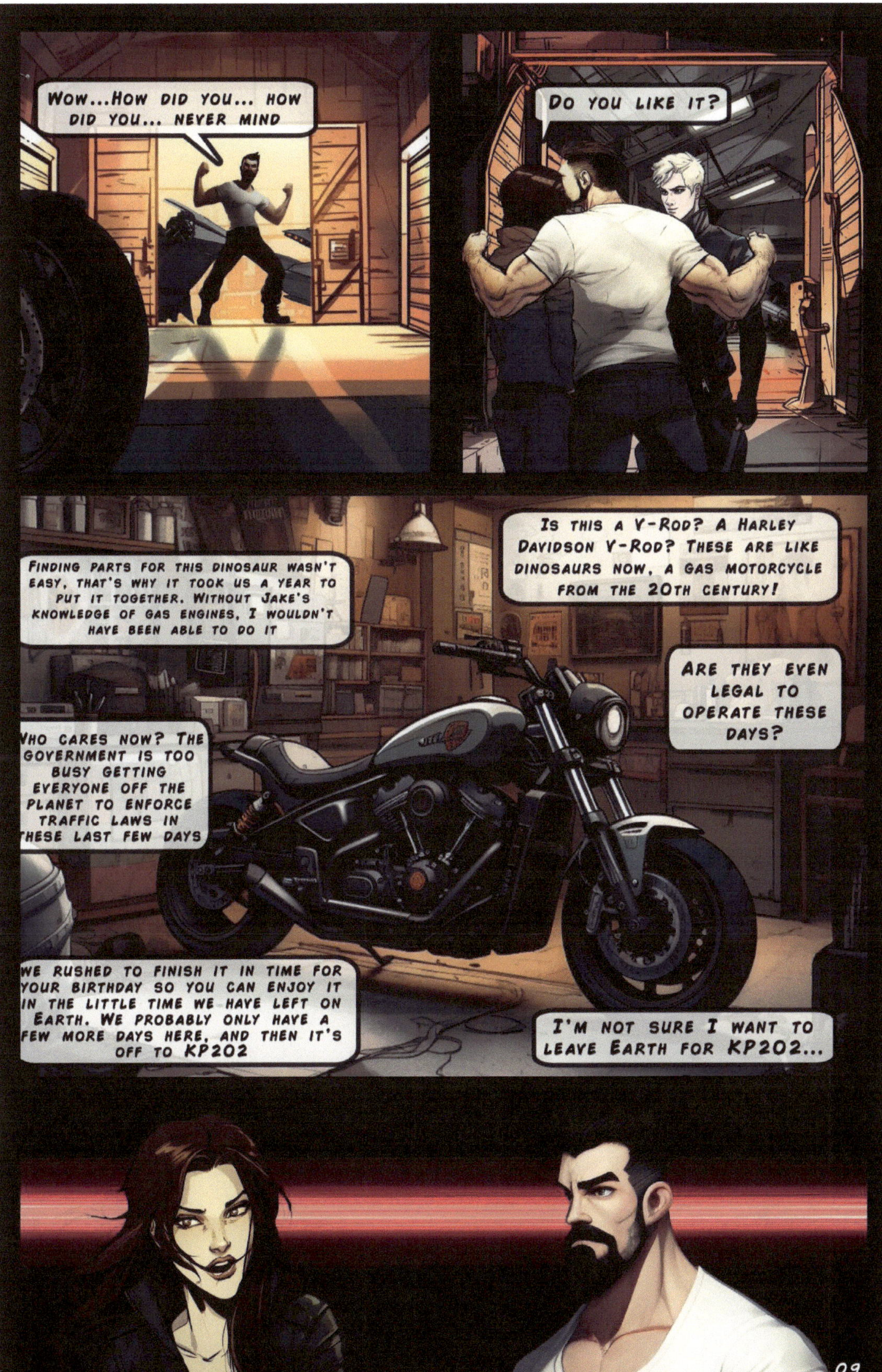
Wow...How did you... how did you... never mind
Do you like it?
Finding parts for this dinosaur wasn't easy, that's why it took us a year to put it together. Without Jake's knowledge of gas engines, I wouldn't have been able to do it
Is this a V-Rod? A Harley Davidson V-Rod? These are like dinosaurs now, a gas motorcycle from the 20th century!
Are they even legal to operate these days?
Who cares now? The government is too busy getting everyone off the planet to enforce traffic laws in these last few days
We rushed to finish it in time for your birthday so you can enjoy it in the little time we have left on Earth. We probably only have a few more days here, and then it's off to KP202
I'm not sure I want to leave Earth for KP202...

DON'T EVEN THINK ABOUT IT! EVERY SINGLE HUMAN BEING WILL BE LEAVING THIS PLANET. HOW WILL YOU SURVIVE? EARTH IS GETTING CLOSER AND CLOSER TO THE SUN. IT WON'T BE A HABITABLE PLACE SOON!

DON'T WORRY, SWEETHEART, NOTHING WILL HAPPEN TO YOUR DAD
EVERYONE WILL LEAVE, DAD. EVERYONE!
NOT EVERYONE. THIS IS OUR HOME. WHERE WOULD I GO? I CANNOT FORSAKE IT.

THIS IS A MESSAGE FROM THE GGC. THE NEXT DEPARTURE FROM EARTH WILL BE IN T-24 HOURS AT SECTOR 38. PLEASE BRING YOUR APPROVED BELONGINGS TO YOUR ASSINGED IP
YOU TWO ARE IN SECTOR 38, CORRECT?
YES, DAD
THEN, IN TWO DAYS' TIME, YOU WILL BE LEAVING
DAD, PROMISE ME YOU'LL JOIN US SOON. YOU'RE IN SECTOR 45
...

YOU'RE A JERK, DAD! A COMPLETE JERK!
EARTH HAS WEATHERED WORSE, BUT AT WHAT COST WHERE ARE ALL THE DINOSAURS NOW? EXTINCT

ADAMU, YOU CAN'T BE SERIOUS. WHAT OF THE BEINGS THAT ARE EMERGING FROM THE FISSURE? THEIR NUMBERS ARE ONLY GROWING, AND IT'S ONLY A MATTER OF TIME BEFORE THEY OVERRUN THE DEFENSES AT THE GREAT FAULT.
ADAM, I IMPLORE YOU TO RECONSIDER THE GRAVITY OF YOUR DECISION
LOVE YOU DAUGHTER. BUT I CANNOT LEAVE BEHIND THE MEMORIES OF YOUR MOTHER, OR ALL THE JOY WE SHARED IN THIS HOME. NO MATTER WHAT, I WILL NOT ABANDON IT

VROOMMM

-CHAPTER 02-
THE DISCOVERY

2052

STARGATE OBSERVATORY, ANCHORAGE, ALASKA

HMM...

HOW BAD IS IT?
HUMANITY'S IN DANGER

THIS ASTEROID IS MASSIVE, AND IS ON A COLLISION COURSE WITH EARTH, IF WE DON'T ACT FAST, IT COULD MEAN THE END OF EVERYTHING WE KNOW
NORMALLY, WHEN A DISCOVERY OF AN ASTEROID IS MADE, IT IS GIVEN THE NAME OF THE DISCOVERER. DAMIAN DIDN'T WANT THAT. HE DIDN'T WANT HIS NAME ATTACHED TO THE KILLER THAT THIS DISCOVERY WAS GOING TO BE
BUT DAMIAN WAS THE MAN THAT SET IT ALL IN MOTION... THAT THE WORLD AS EVERYONE KNEW IT WOULD CHANGE FOREVER FEBRUARY 25TH, 2065

ASTEROID DMN669, AS IT WOULD BE NAMED, CHANGED THINGS BEFORE IT EVER HIT EARTH
2055
A ONE WORLD GOVERNING BODY WAS CREATED, THE GLOBAL GOVERNING COUNCIL, THE G.G.C., AND THE CURRENT PRESIDENT OF THE UNITED STATES, PRESIDENT EDWARDS, EVENTUALLY BECAME ITS FIRST ELECTED LEADER.

2057
One of the first directives for the G.G.C. was to send out ten astronauts, aboard "NOAH'S BIRD", on an exploratory mission to check out a planet that had been discovered several years prior to the asteroid.
G.G.C. NOAH'S BIRD
This planet, KP202, was suspected to be habitable, a twin planet to Earth light years away.

JACK THORINGTON, THE TOP OF HIS CLASS GRADUATE FROM THE UNITED STATES NAVAL ACADEMY, WHO HAD PILOTED MANY SUCCESSFUL MISSIONS TO THE INTERNATIONAL SPACE STATION AND THE MOON, WAS CHOSEN AS THE PILOT AND COMMANDER OF THE MISSION

COSMONAUT YOULISHINKA DIMITROV, A SEASONED PILOT WHO HAD PILOTED MANY RUSSIAN SPACE MISSIONS, WAS SELECTED AS THE SECOND PILOT

LEE CHANG, A MISSION SPECIALIST FROM CHINA WITH 24 MONTHS OF EXPERIENCE ON THE INTERNATIONAL SPACE STATION, WAS IN CHARGE OF OVERALL MISSION SAFETY AND SUCCESS

SAKURA ISHIHARA, A JAPANESE FLIGHT ENGINEER AND ELECTRONIC SYSTEMS SPECIALIST WITH EIGHT MONTHS OF EXPERIENCE IN ORBIT ON THE INTERNATIONAL SPACE STATION, WAS RESPONSIBLE FOR MAINTAINING AND REPAIRING THE SHIP'S EQUIPMENT AND COMPUTER SYSTEMS

ROBERTO BORRELLI, AN ITALIAN CHEMIST AND BIOLOGY SCIENTIST, WAS CHOSEN TO LEAD THE RESEARCH IN HIS FIELD

Elsa Lucas, a launch vehicle control engineer from Sweden, was selected for her expertise in rocket engineering

Jose Perez, a highly skilled avionics specialist from Mexico, was chosen for his technical proficiency in aerodynamics

Doctor Lilith Yosef, an archaeologist and geologist from Israel, was selected for her expertise in geological research

Doctor Carlos López Mosconi, an astrophysicist from Argentina, was chosen to study the celestial bodies in the universe

Doctor Elham Mubarak, a 26 year old physician from Egypt and the youngest team member, was selected for her medical expertise and youthful energy

With a deep breath, Jack set the warp engine to warp-2 speed and pushed the button on his control panel. A wormhole bubble opened up in front of the ship, and in a flash, Noah's Bird was swallowed by it and disappeared. Everything was stretching, warping, bending and distorting. But suddenly the ship's time warp engine whirred to a halt.
Brace yourself, we're about to make history

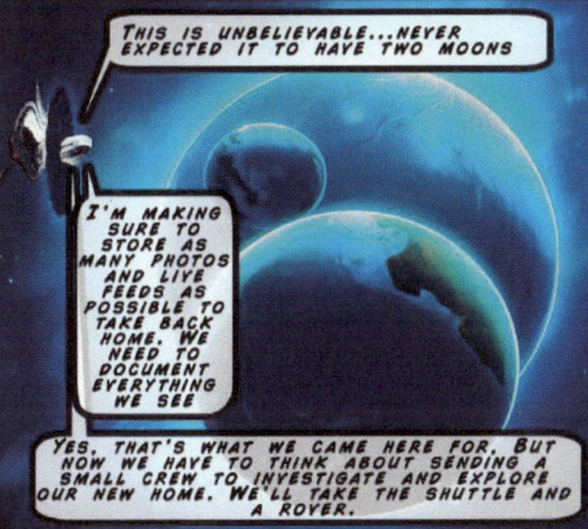

This is unbelievable...never expected it to have two moons
I'm making sure to store as many photos and live feeds as possible to take back home. We need to document everything we see
Yes, that's what we came here for. But now we have to think about sending a small crew to investigate and explore our new home. We'll take the shuttle and a rover.

The team worked tirelessly to ensure everything was in order for the launch. They checked and rechecked all systems, supplies, and equipment. With each passing hour, the excitement grew, until finally, the launch was only minutes away
The mission for the astronauts getting information on KP202 was to last for two years...

…Two grueling years and they didn't know all that they were going to encounter…

The crew of four explored the vast, untamed wilderness of planet KP202, eager to document every inch of this alien world. They marveled at the colorful and unique flora and fauna they encountered along the way, but they also encountered dangerous creatures that tested their courage and survival skills.

...PLANTS AND ANIMALS... CREATURES NEVER SEEN BEFORE...

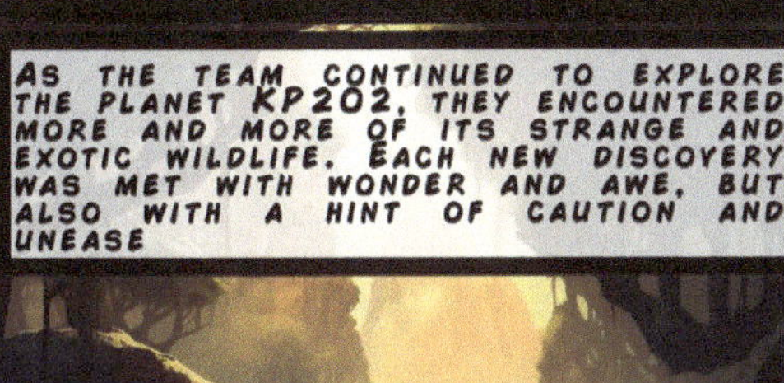
As the team continued to explore the planet KP202, they encountered more and more of its strange and exotic wildlife. Each new discovery was met with wonder and awe, but also with a hint of caution and unease

Wow, look at the size of those things!
Those are called Grazers. They're herbivores, but watch out for their massive tusks. They can be very dangerous if provoked

GRAAARRRR
Oh my god, predators!!

Dr. Borrelli is in the middle of the estampede!

Everyone get down!
It's not working! Just run into the Rover! We must take Dr. to safety!

That was really close, we must be realy cautious in this planet, it isn't safe at all...

As the crew continued their exploration of the planet, they stumbled upon a strange structure buried deep within the dense forests of KP202. The massive stone structure was made of an unknown metal and stood tall, reaching towards the sky. The crew stood in awe at the sight of the ancient ruins, unsure of what they had just uncovered

THIS IS AMAZING!
LET'S SEE IF WE CAN GET INSIDE
LOOK! YOU KNOW WHAT THIS MEANS...
CIVILIZATION..
GUYS... I SEE SOMETHING
..SOMETHING'S NOT RIGHT..
IT JUST FEELS... I DON'T KNOW... LIKE WE'RE NOT ALONE

DEFINITELY CIVILIZATION
WHOA...

WE NEED TO TAKE PICTURES… GET SAMPLES

DO YOU GUYS FEEL LIKE SOMEONE'S WATCHING US?

LOOK OUT! RUN!

GRAAARRRR

WEAPONS, WEAPONS, WEAPONS!!!
LILITH RUN!!!
UH-NO!
..GUK..
NOOOOOOO!
23

BLAM
BLAM
BLAM
GET OUT! GET OUT! GET OUT!
THERE IS THE EXIT, RUN!!! I'LL CARRY LILITH'S BODY

GRAAARRRR
TO THE ROVER!!
JACK, FRIEND, THAT WAS INSANE! WE WERE SUPER LUCKY GETTING OUT OF THAT PLACE. AT LEAST YOU AND I... THIS PLANET ISN'T SAFE AT ALL. WHAT ARE WE GOING TO DO? HUMANITY RELIES ON US..
DOC.. WE NEED TO KEEP THE PUBLIC CONFIDENT IN THE IDEA OF A NEW HABITABLE PLANET, NOT ONE FILLED WITH DANGERS AND MYSTERIES...

-CHAPTER 03-
FIGHTING OUR DEMONS

CHOO
ADAMU! YOU CAME FOR SOME SOUP FOR BREAKFAST?
VROOMMM

NO, THANKS

COME ON, IT'S MY LAST DAY HERE, NOT EVEN A FULL DAY.
CHOO
MY SHIP LEAVES IN A FEW HOURS, AT TEN... UGH, I'M GONNA MISS THIS PLACE. I DON'T EVEN KNOW HOW TO LIVE IN SOME OTHER PLACE... A NEW PLANET?

I GET IT
BUT IF YOU DON'T GO, WHO WOULD MAKE THE PEOPLE ALREADY THERE YOUR FAMOUS SOUP? HUH?!

The old highways and freeways of the 20th century had been transformed into magways powered by electricity, lifting magmobiles and vehicles in an electromagnetic field, rendering petroleum-based transportation obsolete after the great quake. The ruins of the old L.A were left untouched as a living museum of the disaster that devastated much of the old city.

But Adamu wondered how much longer the magways and freeways would remain functional

*** The wall is holding, sir ***
BLAM BLAM BLAM
*** The demons almost broke through, but the rounds stayed them off, pushed them back ***
Major Kelly! Any casualties?
BLAM BLAM BLAM
*** Unfortunately, sir. One hundred dead. Twelve wounded. The first battalion ***
Noticeably, the bullets are not phasing the red demons, their exoskeleton impenetrable to the bullets
BLAM BLAM BLAM
Some are getting to the wall, they're gonna scale it if they do!!
Are the plasma cannons ready?! Bring the plasma cannon, now!
BLAM BLAM BLAM

HURRY! THEY'RE CLIMBING!
THEY'RE COMING! ON MY COMMAND
...
FIRE!!!
SIR! IT WORKED... IT WORKED! THE REMNANTS OF THE RED DEMONS, MOSTLY DISINTEGRATED, A FEW HURT AND INJURED, ARE RETREATING BACK TO THE FAULT LINE!
FOR NOW.

LATER

MAYOR'S OFFICE

JAMES.. MAYOR DALTON...

LT. COLONEL...

So, what can I do for you, Lt. Colonel?
What's the status of the evacuations, sir?
...
The red demons are increasingly becoming more fierce... They're pushing limits, and we're paying the price.
We need to ramp up the evacuation efforts and get people out of here. Soon.
We're building spaceships in underground facilities beneath the city and plan to launch them as soon as they're ready. But even with the fast-track process, it'll take at least two more weeks to start evacuating everyone.
I'm not sure if we have that...

VISITORS ARRIVING
VISITORS ARRIVING
VISITORS ARRIVING
WHO ARE THE VISITORS?
I HAVE IDENTIFIED THE ELECTRONIC SIGNATURE OF YOUR DAUGHTER'S MAGBIKE. THERE IS A COMPANION WITH HER.
OPEN THE DOOR FOR THEM

LOOK, WHO'S HERE... THE TROUBLEMAKERS
CONFUSING US WITH SOMEONE WHO'S NAME STARTS WITH 'A' AND ENDS ... 'U?'
BEER TIME! ANYONE??
THANKS! BUT FEEL FREE LITTLE DAUGHTER'S THIEFT
TOUGH DAY, ADAMU?
HMM. BY THE LOOKS OF IT... WERE YOU SLEEP DAD?
YEAH, I WAS AT THE WALL TODAY. EVERYTIME I'M THERE IT'S... A LOT...
... CONSTANT FIGHTING OFF A HORDE OF RED DEMONS CHARGING AT YOUR LOCATION, TRYING TO RIP EVERYONE TO SHREDS
BUT YOU GUYS WON'T HAVE TO WORRY ABOUT THAT SOON.
DAD, NOT JUST US
MORE AND MORE ARE COMING TO THE SURFACE, LARGE NUMBERS. THEY ATTACKED OUR SOUTHERN DEFENSES. JUST LIKE A FEW WEEKS AGO
LOOK, I KNOW WHAT SECTOR I'M IN... I KNOW WHEN I'M SUPPOSED TO LEAVE ACCORDING TO THAT. BUT MILITARY CAN'T LEAVE UNTIL ALL CIVILIANS ARE EVACUATED, SWEETIE. AND THAT'S THAT.

Good morning big boss!
The next morning
Remember mom used to do this? I used to love to see her dance in the morning... She would play music to start the day
Residents of sectors 35 and 36, proceed to the south section of the city. The doors of arks 503 and 504 are now opening. The arks will launch at 10:00 and 10:30 AM respectively
Okay... I have to go out there and help with the evacuation efforts
Make sure to bring all allotted belongings and be ready for departure. Public pods will be sent to pick up travelers every ten minutes. End of public announcement
An official announcement...
That'll be you guys tomorrow...

EVACUATION SITE
GCC ARK NO 503
GCC ARK NO 504

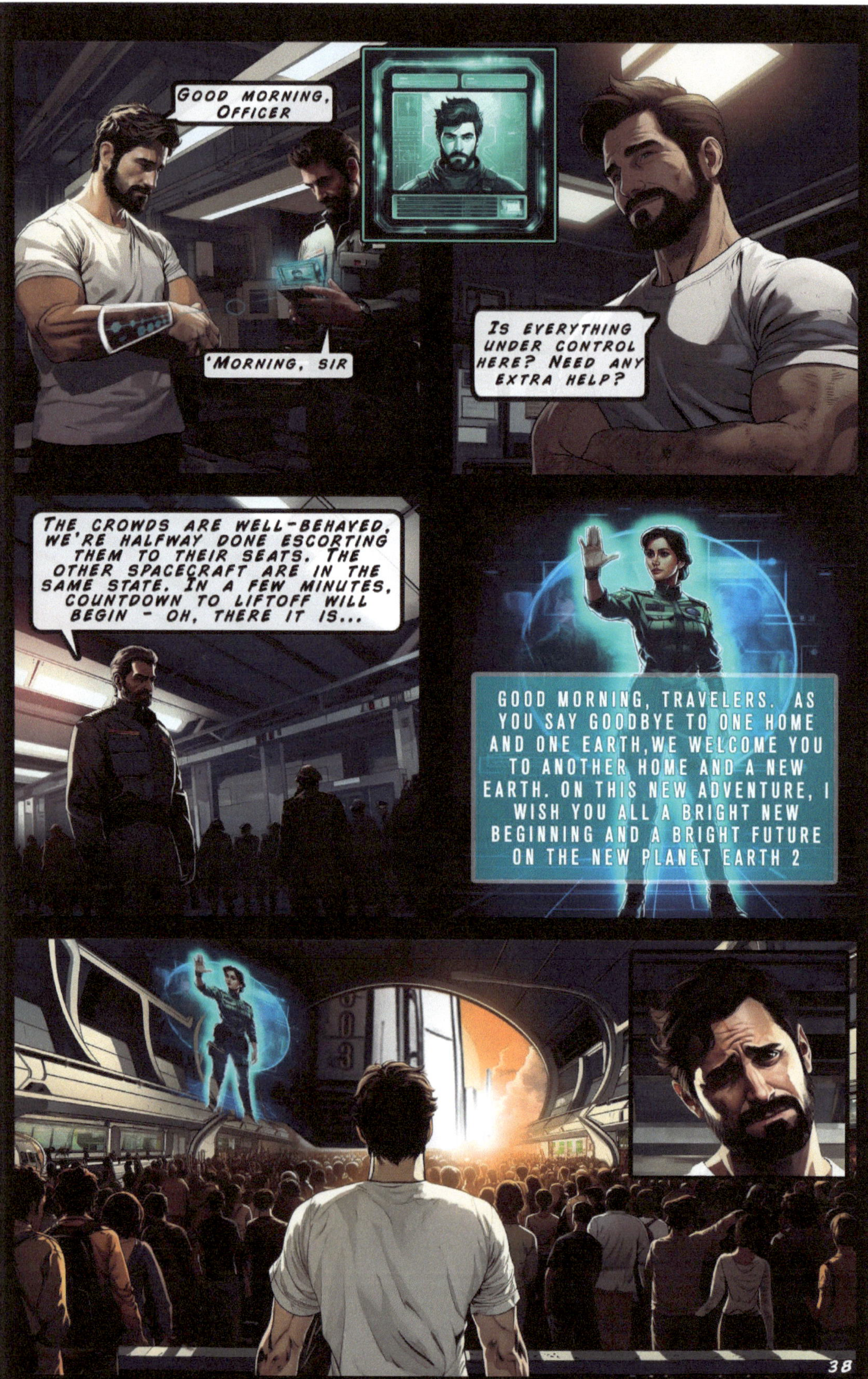
GOOD MORNING, OFFICER
'MORNING, SIR
IS EVERYTHING UNDER CONTROL HERE? NEED ANY EXTRA HELP?
THE CROWDS ARE WELL-BEHAVED. WE'RE HALFWAY DONE ESCORTING THEM TO THEIR SEATS. THE OTHER SPACECRAFT ARE IN THE SAME STATE. IN A FEW MINUTES, COUNTDOWN TO LIFTOFF WILL BEGIN - OH, THERE IT IS...
GOOD MORNING, TRAVELERS. AS YOU SAY GOODBYE TO ONE HOME AND ONE EARTH,WE WELCOME YOU TO ANOTHER HOME AND A NEW EARTH. ON THIS NEW ADVENTURE, I WISH YOU ALL A BRIGHT NEW BEGINNING AND A BRIGHT FUTURE ON THE NEW PLANET EARTH 2

GODSPEED, TRAVELERS...
GODSPEED

VROOMMM
Riding back to his home where his daughter and her fiance waited for him for the last time, Adamu couldn't help but think about his wife.
And now he was only a day away from losing someone else he loved. Ramia.
Dorothy. He had even named his magbike after her. He loved the bike, but he loved her more. It only made sense to name something else you loved the name of what you loved most when it's no longer there for you to love.
And that would just have to be good enough.
But at least this time it wouldn't be like the last. He would know that his daughter was alive... Good... And safe.

MORNING OF RAMIA AND JAKE'S DEPARTURE
W-WHAT'S GOING ON?
I'M THINKING... ONE LAST RIDE ON THIS EARTH? TO THE EVACUATION SITE.
LET'S DO IT!!!
41

VROOMMM
HAHAHA YOU BETTER NOT BE LETTING ME WIN!
VROOMMM
NEVER, SWEETIE... NEVER...
VROOMMM

-CHAPTER 04-
NEW BATTLE

BOOOOOOOOOOOMMMMM

WHAT THE HELL HAPPENED?!?!
UH - HELLO?
THAT!! THAT WAS MY DAUGHTER'S SHIP?! WHAT...
WAIT... WHO ARE YOU?
I'M THE NEW MAYOR... EVETTE DANIEL AND YOU MUST BE LT. COLONEL
ADAMU, YES
THAT WASN'T YOUR DAUGHTER'S SHIP, I ASSURE YOU... BUT THE FORMER MAYOR, FOR THE LACK OF A BETTER WAY TO SAY THIS, FREAKED OUT OVER REPORTS OF A PROJECTED ONSLAUGHT COMING FROM THE RED DEMONS
UNFORTUNATELY, HE AND HIS FAMILY WERE ON THE ARK THAT EXPLODED

He rushed things, pushed that Ark to launch without proper protocols and system checks... Sad, devastating. But your daughter and... fiance? Both are fine.
This is a trying time to begin with and this tragedy is just going to make it all the more difficult. Fear and worry can spread quickly.
I hope I can count of you to do some more heroics, like helping to assuage the people... That they can still trust what we're doing, this Arks, and get them to New Earth.
Of course , Mrs. Mayor.
Eva, please. Friends call me Eva.
Look forward to talking to you more, Lt. Colonel
Just Adamu
And I hope so.
46

LATER... IN THE CONTROL ROOM, AT THE DEFENSIVE POST
KEEP FIRING AT THEM!!!
WE.. WE ARE SIR, BUT THE PLASMA MACHINE GUNS AREN'T STOPPING THEM!
KELLY... CANNONS. I... I KNOW WHAT IT WILL DO TO THE WALL, BUT WE GOTTA GET THOSE THINGS BACK, WE GOTTA STOP THEM.
USE THE CANNONS, THEY'RE FULLY CHARGED. GO!!
ROGER!
KLIK

LT. COLONEL, WH.. WHAT ARE YOU DOING? W.. WHERE ARE YOU GOING?
I'M GONNA DRAW THEM AWAY. BACK TOWARDS THE FAULT LINE.
...BUT SIR...
TELL THE TROOPS TO HANG IN THERE, JUST KEEP THEM AT BAY.
KLIK
I'M ON MY WAY. I'LL USE THE TUNNELS.

VRRRRR
VROOMMM

I'M GETTING CLOSER:
I JUST GOT OUT OF
THE TUNNEL SYSTEM!
KLIK
VRRRRR

VROOMMM

WE'RE STILL FIRING ON THEM, SIR. BUT THEY'RE RIGHT THERE.
KLIK

KEEP FIRING!!!
KLIK

ALL RIGHT, DOROTHY. MAX SPEED!
KLIK
SIR! THERE ARE TWO OF THEM LEFT ON THE WALL!
VRRRRR

GRAAARRRR

I'M THERE!
KLIK

EAT SOME PLASMA!!!
BLAM BLAM BLAM

GRAAARRRR

YES! I MANAGED TO DRAW THEIR ATTENTION JUST LIKE I WANTED! THEY ARE COMING DOWN!!!
KLIK

GOT 'EM. I'MMA LEAD THEM AWAY.
KLIK

VRRRRR

GRAAARRRR

BLAM
BLAM
BLAM

VRRRRR
GRAAARRRR

NOW WE ARE GOING TO HAVE A REAL CONVERSATION...

HASTA LA VISTA...
DEMONS...
FFFFFIIIIUUUUUU

BWWWOOOOOOOOONNN

THHHOOOOOOOMMMM

RRRRRRAAAARGGGHHH
AH... YOU WANT MORE? NO PROBLEM BUDDY!

RRRRRRAAAARGGGHHH

THHHOOOOOOMMMM

THAT WAS AN EPIC BATTLE, SIR
KLIK
KLIK
YEAH...

EAT THAT... MOTHER******

-CHAPTER 05-
A NEW BEGINNING?

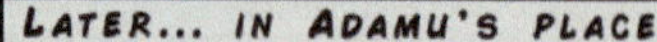

I want to apologize for all the trouble I gave you during my teenage years, with my mood swings and yelling fits. But you never wavered.

I know you promised me you would come to KP202 once all the civilians were off the planet. But something tells me you won't. I can read you, just like Mom could.

If you're going to stay, I know you promised me you'll be okay, but please stay safe. You can use any equipment, electronic or otherwise, that Jake and I amassed over the years in the garage or the apartment.

... ONE MORE THING, DAD. I WAS WORKING ON A DEVICE THAT CAN SEND A SIGNAL TO KP202 USING MORSE CODE-LIKE SIGNALS. IT'S SIMILAR TO SENDING THINGS VIA TIME WARP, BUT THE SIGNALS GET THROUGH IN HOURS OR DAYS, INSTEAD OF TAKING THOUSANDS OF YEARS ...

HOW THINGS CHANGE...
VRRRRR
CHOO
...NOTHING EVER STAYS THE SAME...
HEY-HEY.. C-COME HERE.. SMMH SMMH.. COME HERE
ARE YOU LOST BUDDY? LET'S SEE WHO IS MISSING YOU..
EVETTE LARA
DANIEL

THE NEXT DAY...

PERFECT. WE HAVE THE NEXT 50 LAUNCHES, DATES, ALL SQUARED AWAY WITH MAINTENANCE SCHEDULED FOR CHECKS.

THAT'S A TOTAL OF 100 THIS MONTH. THAT'S OVER 200,000 PEOPLE EVACUATED AND SAFE.
WHAT'S NEXT ON THE LIST?

LUCY WAS MY DAD'S LAST BIRTHDAY GIFT TO ME WHEN HE PASSED AWAY THREE YEARS AGO.

OKAY...

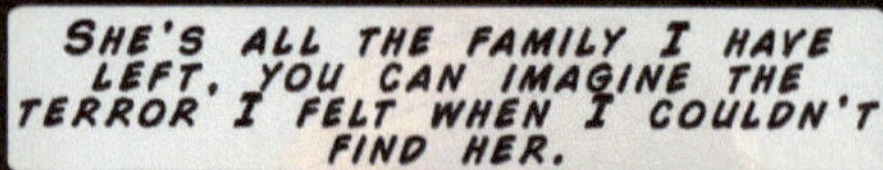
SHE'S ALL THE FAMILY I HAVE LEFT, YOU CAN IMAGINE THE TERROR I FELT WHEN I COULDN'T FIND HER.

THE ELECTRONIC TRACKER ON HER COLLAR ALWAYS WORKS, BUT THIS ONE TIME WHEN I NEEDED IT MOST, IT MALFUNCTIONED. WHEN MY APARTMENT'S A.I. DETECTED LUCY'S COLLAR, I RAN OUTSIDE LIKE A CRAZY PERSON.

AND THERE HE WAS...

LT. COLONEL ADAMU... AND I CAN'T GET HIM OFF MY MIND.

THEN YOU SHOULD ASK HIM OUT. DON'T WASTE ANY TIME... WE NO LONGER HAVE THAT LUXURY.

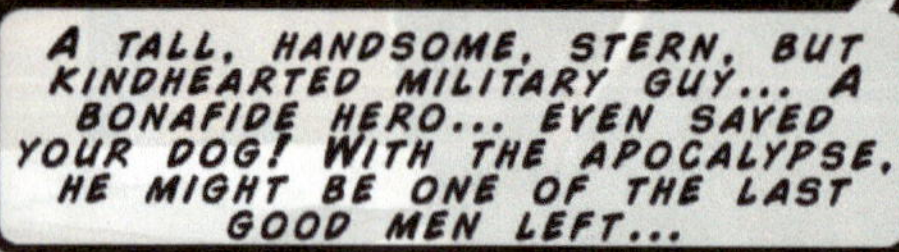
A TALL, HANDSOME, STERN, BUT KINDHEARTED MILITARY GUY... A BONAFIDE HERO... EVEN SAVED YOUR DOG! WITH THE APOCALYPSE, HE MIGHT BE ONE OF THE LAST GOOD MEN LEFT...

...
...YOU BETTER MAKE YOUR MOVE.

THAT NIGHT

KNOCK KNOCK!!

OK!! COMING!! OH...

I KNOW THIS WAS IMPROMPTU, BUT I'M GLAD YOU WERE SO... AH, ACCOMMODATING WHEN I CALLED.

SHOCKED... AND A PLEASANT SURPRISE

I WANTED TO PROPERLY THANK YOU FOR SAVING THE DAY

NOT YOUR HEROICS WITH THE RED DEMONS... BUT MY DOG

HA! OF COURSE, GOOD TO KNOW.

LATER
...YES, SO LUCY IS BEING DOGGY-SAT TONITE BY MY SECRETARY AND GOOD FRIEND, JANE... WHO BY THE WAY CONVINCED ME TO CALL YOU FOR THIS.
WELL, THANK YOU TO JANE... AND TO LUCY FOR GOING MISSING.
IT'S FUNNY... WHEN I WENT TO MR. CHOO'S RESTAURANT THE OTHER NIGHT IT WAS BECAUSE I WAS REALLY FEELING LONELY
OH, I'M SO SORRY, I...
WITH RAMIA AND JAKE GONE... HM.. MR. CHOO'S WAS WHERE MY WIFE AND I HAD OUR FIRST DATE.
NO NO NO... DON'T.. DON'T BE!

I'M ENJOYING THIS MOMENT.
I'M GLAD I WENT. I'M GLAD I FELT LONELY... IT LED M TO LUCY WHICH THE LED ME TO YOU AN THAT'S HOW WE GO HERE... TO THIS MOMENT.
TO ENJOYING THIS MOMENT!!
KLINCK!
BUT SERIOUS...
...VERY SORRY ABOUT YOUR WIFE.
THANK YOU. IT'S BEEN A WHILE THOUGH...

So, what about you?
Well, no Mr. Right for me.. Not yet... But yeah... I've been busy with my education and career, and for the past few years, I've been taking care of my father. There have been a few men here and there, but nothing serious enough to hang my hat on.
My mom left me and my dad when I was five and no one's ever seen her again. I guess she wasn't too thrilled about being tied down by family.
But my dad's always been there for me, just like you assumed the role of both father and mother for Ramia after your wife passed.
Hnn...
Another glass?
Uh... Oh my! I wish I could, but I, I can't. Some meetings tomorrow morning.
Oh oh oh, yeah, of course. I walk you to the door..

I REALLY ENJOYED THIS.

I ENJOYED SPENDING TIME WITH YOU... GETTING TO KNOW YOU.

ME TOO...

HAVE A GOOD NIGHT, LT. COLONEL.

...I'LL TRY...

-CHAPTER 06-
NEW EARTH

BOOOOOOOOOOOMMMM

BWWWOOOOOOOONNN

Wake up...
Hey, Ramia,
honey... Wake-
Huh-?!
You were
dreaming
about the
crash again?
Yeah... It-It was so intense.
I'm just grateful we made
it, not everyone did.
Hnn. Yeah...
Come on. Come
see this.
What are
you talking
about?
Come on, I'll
show you.
W-What is it?
Well, it's
ours...
Hey. Got all
your guy's
stuff!!!

SELF-DEFENSE...? FOR WHAT JAKE??

SELF DEFENSE

WHOA..

I-I DON'T UNDERSTAND... WHY DO WE NEED SO MANY WEAPONS? AND THESE KINDS OF WEAPONS? THIS IS PRETTY HEAVY-DUTY STUFF.

MAYBE BECAUSE THIS PLANET ISN'T THE UTOPIA EVERYONE HAS MADE IT OUT TO ...

OFFICIALLY... JACK THORINGTON.
FROM NOAH'S BIRD, THE FIRST SHIP HERE, EXPLORATORY MISSION. YOU'RE A HERO.
I DON'T KNOW ABOUT THAT. BUT THE FACT IS, KP202 WAS OUR ONLY HOPE FOR SURVIVAL. THE GOVERNMENT KNEW ABOUT THE DANGERS, BUT THEY SAW NO OTHER OPTION.
WE HAD TO FIND A NEW HOME BEFORE IT WAS TOO LATE. YOU'LL NEED TO BE ON YOUR GUARD AT ALL TIMES. THE CREATURES HERE ARE UNLIKE ANYTHING YOU'VE EVER ENCOUNTERED.
AND THE LANDSCAPE CAN BE JUST AS TREACHEROUS, WITH HAZARDOUS TERRAIN AND UNPREDICTABLE WEATHER PATTERNS...
BUT WITH THE RIGHT TRAINING AND EQUIPMENT, YOU CAN THRIVE HERE.
NOW, IF YOU'LL EXCUSE ME, I HAVE SOME WORK TO DO. BUT DON'T HESITATE TO COME FIND ME IF YOU NEED ANYTHING.
DEFINITELY,THANK YOU!!

I GUESS THERE'S A POSSIBILITY THIS PLANET MIGHT NOT ONLY BE PLAGUED WITH GIANT PREDATORS... BASED ON THE EXPLORATORY MISSION, HE CAN'T GUARANTEE THAT THERE AREN'T INTELLIGENT CREATURES HERE, TOO, RIGHT?
YEAH, I GUESS. I MEAN, WE COULD BE THE INVADING ALIENS. WHAT WOULD YOU HAVE DONE IF YOU SAW THOUSANDS OF MASSIVE SPACESHIPS LANDING ON EARTH, CARRYING THOUSANDS OF EXTRATERRESTRIAL BEINGS? WE WOULD HAVE FOUGHT THEM, RIGHT?
WE NEED TO STAY VIGILANT AND ALWAYS HAVE A WEAPON ON HAND.
BUT I DO APPRECIATE JACK THORINGTON BEING UPFRONT ABOUT THE DANGERS OF THIS PLANET. THE G.G.C. HAD NO CHOICE BUT TO TELL US HALF TRUTHS. WHAT ELSE COULD THEY DO? TELL THE PEOPLE THAT THEY'RE ESCAPING A DYING EARTH, ONLY TO COME TO A PLANET WITH ITS OWN VICIOUS CREATURES?
THE EARTH WAS GETTING CLOSER AND CLOSER TO THE SUN, EVERYTHING WAS GOING TO BE SCORCHED SOON.
YEAH, BUT WE DON'T KNOW THAT FOR SURE... BUT THEY NEVER MENTIONED THE DANGERS OF THIS NEW PLANET. MAYBE THEY SHOULD HAVE, SO PEOPLE COULD MAKE AN INFORMED DECISION.
I'M STARTING TO THINK YOUR DAD WAS RIGHT TO STAY BEHIND.
ADAMU IS A FOOL IF HE THINKS HE CAN BEAT THE ODDS BY FIGHTING A LOSING BATTLE.
I'M SO SORRY, I DIDN'T MEAN IT. I'M SURE ADAMU WILL BE OKAY AND WILL BE ON ONE OF THESE SHIPS SOON. LET'S JUST BE CAREFUL ON THIS NEW PLANET, OKAY?
OKAY...

How are my two beloved today?
Weeks later...
Hey honey! Hello!
I'm sorry love, I was in my world
Stay vigilant, right? Make sure you have this next to you just in case.
Right, just in case...
Okay baby, I'll go on with my duties
CHUICK
What was that?!
RAMIA!!!

RAMIA! RAMIA!
LOOK-LOOK OUT!

MOVE! MOVE!
RAMIA!

JAKE? WHAT'S
GOING ON?
BEHIND YOU!
BEHIND YOU!

HUH...

RRRRRAAAAARGGGGH

NOOOOOOOOO!

BWWWOOOOOOOONNN

VRAAAKKKK

JAKE... NO...
PL-PLEASE,
GOD, NO...

-CHAPTER 07-
BACK ON EARTH

AND THEN THE END CAME. AGAIN.
GO TO HELL DEMON!
CITIZENS OF NEW L.A., HEAD TO THE NEAREST SHELTER. CREATURES HAVE ESCAPED THE CITY DEFENSES, THE CITY IS BEING OVERRUN.
BWWWOOOOOOOOONNN
RRRRRRAAAARGGGHHH
KLIK
KELLY, WHAT DO WE GOT?
IT'S BAD. WORST ONE YET. LT. COLONEL. WE'RE TRYING TO GET THE LAST FEW ARKS UP AND READY, BUT WE STILL NEED A FEW DAYS.
KLIK
OKAY, OKAY... I'LL DO MY BEST TO CLEAR SOME OUT, MAJOR.
THANK YOU, SIR.
I-I GOTTA GO. HAVE TO PICK UP MY MAG..
BUT THIS TIME THERE WAS NO TIME FOR PREPARATION
KLIK
ADAMU, THEY'RE-THEY'RE EVERYWHERE! EVERYTHING IS -
EVE!!! I'M ON MY WAY. FIND SOME PLACE SAFE. HIDE.
VROOMMM
THIS WAS SURVIVAL...

A RACE TO THE END.
WHAT THE ...
VROOMMM

KLIK
EVE!!! EVA! EVA, COME IN.. PLEASE!!
ADAMU!

OH MY GOD-!

H-HOLD ON. I'MMA GET YOU OUT.

EVA- OH NO ... OH ... LUCY.. SH**. WHAT A MESS
NOW YOU ARE SAFE HONEY, I'LL TAKE CARE OF YOU

LATER
YOU'RE SAFE HERE... WITH ME. IS THERE ANYTHING I CAN GET YOU?
LUCY... SHE WAS BARKING AND NUDGING ME ALONG. SHE WAS DOING HER BEST TO SAVE ME... SAVE US.
I'M SORRY...
I.. I DON'T WANT TO BE ALONE...
... NOT TONIGHT. MAYBE NOT EVER AGAIN.

DAYS LATER
EVEN IN THE END THERE ARE REPRIEVES, MOMENTS WHERE YOU CAN PRETEND THAT LIFE IS NORMAL, THAT IT'S NOT ENDING.
THESE ARE THE MOMENTS THAT YOU FIGHT FOR.
I'M GLAD I'M HERE.
ME TOO
NO MATTER HOW SHORT THEY ARE.
LAST EVACUATIONS
PREPARING
LAST EVACUATIONS ARE NOW PREPARING!
LAST EVACUATIONS ARE NOW PREPARING!
LAST EVACUATIONS ARE NOW PREPARING!
LAST EVACUATIONS ARE NOW PREPARING!
I GUESS THAT'S US...
85

...
I'M NOT GOING.
WHAT?!
I JUST CAN'T LEAVE THIS BEHIND...
THEN...
I'M STAYING TOO.
I CAN'T ASK YOU TO...
YOU DIDN'T ASK ME. I FOUND YOU, AND I'M NOT LOSING YOU...

LATER THAT NIGHT.
THIS IDEA OF YOURS...
IF WE ARE BOTH STAYING, THEN WE NEED TO KNOW WHAT WE'RE UP AGAINST.
SO WHAT? WE DISSECT ONE OF THESE THINGS???
YEAH, TO UNDERSTAND THEM, BIOLOGY, THEIR PHYSIOLOGY. THERE MAY BE SOMETHING THERE WE CAN USE.
THERE!! BY THE ALLEY
IT'S LOADED HONEY!! NOW SECURE IT IN THE MAGTRUCK!!
WHAT ARE WE UP AGAINST, ADAMU? LOOK AT THIS THING. DO WE EVEN STAND A CHANCE?
LOCK N' LOAD! LET'S GO BACK TO THE GARAGE

AT ADAMU'S GARAGE, THEY HAVE LEARNED A MASSIVE AMOUNT OF INFORMATION ABOUT THE CREATURE...
OK HONEY, SO... ITS SHELL IS AS HARD AS A ROCK... BUT ONCE WE GET IT OPEN...
...AN EXOSKELETON WITH TWO SHELLS. THE OUTERMOST SHELL IS COVERED IN IRON OXIDE AND STRONTIUM.
IRON OXIDE AND TRACE STRONTIUM REACT WITH OXYGEN AND WATER VAPOR IN THE AIR, GIVING THESE CREATURES THEIR INTENSE RED COLOR... SORRY, BIOLOGY AND CHEMISTRY BACKGROUND, HERE.
ROGER THAT... LOOK - THE OUTER SHELL OF THIS CREATURE IS MADE OF TITANIUM-CARBIDE AND HAFNIUM-CARBIDE, NO WONDER IT CAN WITHSTAND TEMPERATURES OVER 4000 DEGREES CELSIUS. NO WONDER THEY CAN LIVE IN THE INTENSE HEAT DEEP IN THE EARTH.
IT'S MADE OF CARBON-CARBON WITH REINFORCED FIBERS, IT PROBABLY HAS A STRENGTH OF UP TO 700 MPA AND CAN KEEP THAT STRENGTH EVEN AT 2000 DEGREES CELSIUS. THESE CREATURES ARE TOUGH, LIKE ARMORED VEHICLES.
AND THERE - THE LUNGS IN THE BACK ARE MORE RED, WHILE THE ONES IN FRONT ARE MORE BLACK. THE RED ONES LOOK THINNER, TOO. THE BLOOD FROM THE RED LUNGS HAS A THINNER CONSISTENCY AND IS REDDISH BROWN, WHILE THE BLOOD FROM THE BLACK LUNGS IS THICKER AND BLACK. THAT MEANS IT HAS TWO CIRCULATORY SYSTEMS, EACH WITH A DIFFERENT TYPE OF BLOOD.

(Eva) ..This also means that these creatures are designed for both environments. They can live both above ground and deep beneath the earth, where there's high levels of sulfur, methane gas, and iron. One for the surface and one for the depths.
(Adamu) When they're deep beneath the earth, their surface circulatory system probably goes dormant, as it's not needed. But when they come to the surface, the surface circulatory system is reactivated and slowly becomes functional, while the other goes dormant and gradually deactivates..
(Adamu) ..That's probably why the red lungs are smaller now, but if the theory is correct, the red lungs that will breathe oxygen will become larger over time and the other ones will become smaller. That makes perfect sense. That's why when these creatures first emerged from underground, they were in a daze and didn't wander too far from the great fault. But as they spent more time on the surface, they started to adapt to the new atmosphere and became bolder and stronger. That's when they started attacking us..
(Adamu) ..Know what else this means? This isn't the first time these creatures have come to the surface. They probably emerged hundreds of thousands or even millions of years ago and wiped out any existing human or animal life. Ever heard Gargoyles?

WHAT NOW!?
MAJOR KELLLY
OK DOROTHY, ACCEPT THE COMMUNICATION
COMMS ARE FALLING DOWN, THIS IS MAJOR KELLY, SIR! WE ARE RECEIVING A LOT OF NOISE, IT'S ONLY A MATTER OF TIME UNTIL WE GO OFFLINE!
KLIK
THE CITY IS COMPLETELY OVERRUN. THE LAST ARKS ARE PREPARED TO LAUNCH. ARE YOU AND THE MAYOR SURE ABOUT YOUR DECISION?
WE ARE.

-CHAPTER 08-
SURVIVAL OF THE FITTEST

NEW L.A. IS COMPLETELY OVERRUN BY THE RED DEMONS.
RRRRRRAAAARGGGHHH

PWEEN
PWEEN
PWEEN

GRAAARRRR

THE LAST SPACHESHIP WAS LAUNCHED INTO SPACE, THERE WAS NO POSIBLE WAY TO LAUNCH ANOTHER ONE. THE STRUCTURES OF THE REBUILT CITY HAYE FALLEN AND THE END OF EYERYTHING IS NEAR...

SEVERAL WEEKS LATER, IN A STEEL-REINFORCED SAFE ROOM...
LIFE HAS ALWAYS BEEN ABOUT THE SURVIVAL OF THE FITTEST.
AND DESPITE THE TRAJECTORY OF HUMAN EVOLUTION, THE SIMPLE FACT REMAINS THE SAME.
ALMOST GONE, HUN.
THE WATER?
DIDN'T ACCOUNT FOR THEM BUSTING THE FILTRATION SYSTEM, NO CLEAN WATER IS A PROBLEM.
HNN. YEAH IT IS...
...BUT WE'LL FIND A WAY.
WE WILL.
I KNOW. I'M WITH YOU.

I MAY HAVE TO VENTURE OUT...
NOT WITHOUT ME.
... A FEW LESSONS BEFORE LEAVING THE SAFE ROOM ...
OK HONEY, LET'S GO UPSTAIRS
EVERYTHING IS DESTRUCTION, THE PASSAGE OF DEMONS LEAVES ITS MARK...

DISTRIBUTION CENTER
OVER THERE!
WE'LL GRAB WHATEVER WE CAN, WHATEVER IS LEFT... BUT ESPECIALLY WATER.
HERE WE HAVE BEANS IN GOOD CONDITION AND BOTTLES OF WATER, PUT THEM IN THE BAG EVE.
SHIT, DID YOU HEAR THAT??
THEY'RE IN THE STORE!
CLANK!
HONEY RUN!! LEAVE THE BACKPACK, WE MUST HIDE AT THE BACK!!
RRRRRRAAAARGGGHHH

RRRRRRAAAARGGGHHH

LOOK! THE COLD CHAMBER!
GET IN QUICK!!

SHHH...

SNIFF
SNIFF

SNIFF
SNIFF
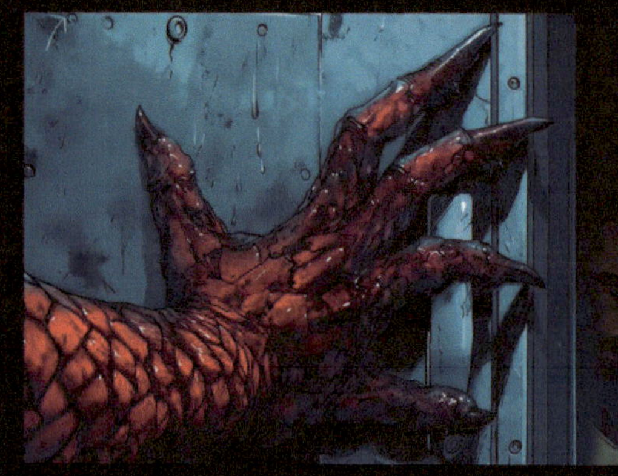

IIIIIJJJGGGGKKK

WAIT... THEY RAN AWAY. WHY?
REMEMBER THEIR TWO SHELLS? THINK EXOSKELETON AND ENVIRONMENT... MAYBE THEY DON'T LIKE THE COLD...
ME NEITHER, IT'S FREEZING HERE, LET'S GO OUT!

HOURS LATER
HERE IS THE GASOLINE BABE, DO YOU REALLY THINK THIS WILL WORK?
AND WHY NOT THE MAGBIKE.
I DO, AND THE ELECTRICAL GRID SYSTEM HAS BEEN COMPROMISED, THE CONSTANT POWER FLUCTUATIONS WILL RENDER THE MAGWAYS USELESS AND MAKE IT DIFFICULT TO ESCAPE THE DEMONS.
I MUST FINISH MODIFYING THIS BEAUTY, AND THEN IF WE MAKE IT TO ALASKA... SOMEPLACE COLD, WE HAVE A CHANCE.
I'M WITH YOU.

VRRRRR
TRYING TO OUTRUN THE INEVITABLE, THAT IS THE PLIGHT OF HUMAN EXISTENCE.

SIMPLY BECAUSE WE KNOW THAT THERE IS AN END.

THE SURVIVALIST IN HUMANITY MAKES US REACH OUT AND PURSUE THE IMPOSSIBLE BECAUSE IT SEEMS PLAUSIBLE...

YOU READY TO FREEZE THOSE BASTARDS??

LIQUID NITROGEN SPRAY, CHECK. READY AS I EVER WILL BE.

...TO JUST LIVE.
I THINK IT'S WORKING!

EAT THIS ICE ROCK!!
PWEEN
VRAAAKKKK
SSHHOOOOOSHH
RRRRRRAAAARGGGHHH
THERE ARE TOO MANY, WE MUST ESCAPE!
GO ON HONEY!! WE ARE LEAVING THEM BEHIND
VRRRRR
SSHHOOOOOSHH

AAAAAAAAA!!!
WHAT THE HELL??
WAIT HERE BABE, I'LL CHECK
HELPPPP!!!!
EAT THIS MOTHER*****!!
T-TAKE HER... PL-PLEASE... I CAN'T GO ON...
I'M GOING TO TAKE CARE OF HER AS IF SHE WERE MINE, TAKE IT FOR GRANTED.

THE JOURNEY FOR A SAFEHOUSE STARTED. AS THE NEW FAMILY ADVANCED, THE PRESENCE OF DEMONS WAS DIMINISHING.

THE NEED FOR SAVING FUEL WAS HIGHER, AND THE Y-ROD WAS TOO HEAVY TO CONTINUE CARRYING WEAPONS WITH NO APPARENT USE.

ITH EVERY MILE THEY MADE, THE OLDER IT GOT, SO THEY BECAME ASTERS OF SCAVENGING PLACES FOR ARMER CLOTHES AND RATIONS.

THE BABY NEVER BECAME A BURDEN. ON THE CONTRARY, IT STRENGTHENED FAMILY TIES.

KLINCK!
HEY HONEY! WHAT'S GOING ON?
I HEARD A NOISE COMING FROM HERE...
P-PLEASE LET ME GO... THOSE THINGS W-WERE GONE DAYS AGO, B-BUT I CAN'T HOLD ON A-ANOTHER SECOND...
..SHIT..
GO BACK TO SLEEP BABE, I'LL TAKE CARE OF IT
BLAM

(1) DEAR DAD, I HOPE THIS MESSAGE FINDS YOU WELL AND THAT YOU MANAGED TO SURVIVE THE DEMON APOCALYPSE. IF YOU ARE ABLE TO RECEIVE THIS, I IMPLORE YOU TO REPLY AS SOON AS POSSIBLE. JUST THE THOUGHT OF KNOWING THAT YOU ARE SAFE WOULD BRING ME IMMENSE COMFORT.

(2) THE COLONISTS ON THE NEW PLANET KP202, INCLUDING MYSELF, HAVE FACED COUNTLESS CHALLENGES SINCE OUR ARRIVAL. I AM WRITING TO YOU WITH A HEAVY HEART, AS I BEAR THE DEVASTATING NEWS OF JAKE'S PASSING. HE BRAVELY GAVE HIS LIFE TO PROTECT ME FROM THE DANGERS THAT LURK ON THIS NEW PLANET.

(3) I AM NOW A MOTHER, AND YOU ARE A PROUD GRANDPARENT. I NAMED MY SON JAKE, AFTER HIS FATHER. HE IS NOW FOUR MONTHS OLD AND JUST AS INQUISITIVE AS HIS DAD WAS. I SEE A LOT OF YOU IN HIM.

(4) AS THE DAYS GO BY, MORE AND MORE COLONISTS ARE FALLING ILL FROM UNDIAGNOSED DISEASES, OR BEING HUNTED DOWN BY THESE MASSIVE PREDATORS. AND NOW, WE FACE AN EVEN DEADLIER ENEMY - THE GRAYS. THESE INDIGENOUS HUMANOID-LIKE CREATURES LIVE IN VAST UNDERGROUND CITIES, AS THEY SEEK TO AVOID THE DANGERS OF THE SURFACE. PALE GRAY IN COLOR, THEY POSSESS TWO LARGE EYES AND A MINIMAL NOSE AND MOUTH. DESPITE THEIR SMALL STATURE, THEY ARE INCREDIBLY INTELLIGENT AND HAVE WEAPONS THAT RIVAL OURS. THEY CONSIDER US INVADING ALIENS, COMPETING FOR RESOURCES AND FOOD, AND THEY ATTACK US AT NIGHT. NO ONE HAS RETURNED TO TELL US WHAT HAPPENS TO THOSE WHO ARE CAPTURED....

(5) You were right, Dad. We gave up too soon on our beloved Earth. Instead of banding together and fighting to save it, we took the easy way out and fled to another planet. But it's not as simple as just taking over. The daily toll of the deaths of the colonists is overwhelming, and I can no longer bear the thought of you being in danger or in need of help on Earth.
Months later.
...And I will huff and puff and blowwww your house do...
(6) I am not alone in my thinking. Many colonists, including my neighbor Jack Hayward Thorington, are also considering a return to Earth. Jack was the captain of the exploration mission that was sent to KP202 on the Noah's Bird. We are planning to sneak into one of the shuttle Arks, and have Jack pilot us back to Earth.
Here ya go...
(7) We understand that our plan is filled with dangers and uncertainties. We may face death at the hands of the red demons or the scorching temperatures, but we would rather die fighting for our home planet than being invaders on an alien planet.

THE ASTEROID'S IMPACT HAS SHIFTED THE PLANET'S ORBIT, CAUSING IT TO ENTER A DEEP ICE AGE. THE SUN IS DISTANT, ONLY REACHING THE PLANET WITH A FEW HOURS OF SUNLIGHT EACH DAY.
THE RED DEMONS HAVE RETURNED TO THE BOWELS OF EARTH FROM WHENCE THEY CAME, HAVING EXTERMINATED MUCH OF THE REMAINING LIFE ON THE PLANET.
IT REMAINS UNCERTAIN IF ANY HUMANS HAVE SURVIVED, BUT IF THEY HAVE, THEY'RE CONFRONTED WITH FREEZING TEMPERATURES AND A DESPERATE STRUGGLE FOR SURVIVAL.
NEW ENDINGS AND OLD BEGINNINGS
(8) I LOVE YOU, DAD, AND I PRAY THAT WE WILL BE REUNITED SOON. UNTIL THEN, TAKE CARE. WITH LOVE, RAMIA (AND BABY JAKE)
THE END

www.ingramcontent.com/pod-product-compliance
Lightning Source LLC
Chambersburg PA
CBHW040823050726
47507CB00021B/108
* 9 7 9 8 9 8 8 6 0 2 5 4 5 *